Superhero HARRY

The Breaktime Bully

by Rachel Ruiz

illustrated by Steve May

raintree 🍃

Raintree is an imprint of Capstone Global Library Limited, a company incorporated in England and Wales having its registered office at 264 Banbury Road, Oxford, OX2 7DY Registered company number: 6695582

www.raintree.co.uk
myorders@raintree.co.uk

ISBN 978 1 4747 4203 0
21 20 19 18 17
10 9 8 7 6 5 4 3 2 1

British Library Cataloguing in Publication Data
A full catalogue record for this book is available from the British Library.

Designed by Hilary Wacholz

Printed and bound in China.

CONTENTS

ALL ABOUT
Superhero
HARRY

NAME: Harrison Albert Cruz

FAVOURITE COLOUR: red

FAVOURITE FOOD: spaghetti

FAVOURITE SCHOOL SUBJECT: science

HOBBIES: playing video games, inventing and reading

IDOLS: Albert Einstein and Superman

BEST FRIEND, NEIGHBOUR, AND SIDEKICK: Macy

LATEST INVENTION: Superhero Flashlight Belt

CHAPTER 1

HARRY'S SUPER HALLOWEEN COSTUME

Harry can't wait to get to school today! It's Halloween! There's going to be a party and a fancy dress parade around school.

Harry's dressing up as Superman. His costume is almost complete. He's wearing his favourite red superhero cape from his aunt Gwen. Now he's just adding the last finishing touch.

Harry loves superheroes. He wishes he had superpowers. If he had superpowers, he probably wouldn't be so clumsy.

But since he doesn't, he builds inventions to make himself more superhero-ish.

His latest invention is his superhero flashlight belt. He made it using one of his old belts, small flashlights, and rubber bands. When he presses a button, the flashlights turn on. It helps Harry find things.

"There it is!" Harry yells, reaching for his superhero mask under his bed.

When Harry gets on the school bus, a girl dressed up as Wonder Woman waves him over.

"Harry, over here!"

That's Macy. She is Harry's next-door neighbour, superhero sidekick, classmate, and best friend.

As Harry walks up to Macy, he trips on his cape. His apple rolls right out of his lunch bag and under a seat.

"Your apple!" Macy says.

"Not to worry," Harry says. "I'll find it with this."

Harry presses the button, and his superhero flashlight belt lights up. He finds the apple in a flash.

"Wow!" Macy says. "You really are like a superhero."

CHAPTER 2

THE NEW KID AT SCHOOL

At Parker Primary School everyone's wearing Halloween costumes. Melanie is a mermaid. Jackson is a cowboy.

Even Ms Lane is wearing a costume. She is dressed like Dorothy from *The Wizard of Oz*. She's wearing ruby slippers and carrying a basket with a cute dog inside.

"Class," Ms Lane says, "we have a new child joining us today. Please say hello to Jeremy."

"Hi, Jeremy!" the class says.

Jeremy is not wearing a costume. And he doesn't look very happy.

"Hey, Jeremy, where's your costume?" Harry asks. "Are you going to put it on after lunch?"

"What are you going to be?" Macy asks.

Jeremy's response surprises Harry and Macy.

"Costumes are lame. Halloween is lame. And this school is super lame," he says, sliding down in his seat.

"Today is your first day at Parker Primary School," Macy says. "How do you know you won't like it here?"

"Just a feeling I get," Jeremy says. He looks at Harry. "What are you supposed to be anyway?"

"I'm Superman, of course!" Harry says proudly, pretending to flex his super muscles.

"His nickname is Superhero Harry," Macy explains. "And Superman is his favourite superhero."

"Superhero Harry? More like Superlame Harry!" Jeremy says as he laughs.

"Hey, that's mean," Macy says, but Jeremy turns his back to her.

Harry and Macy look at each other. Harry just shrugs.

CHAPTER 3

THE BREAKTIME BULLY

At breaktime things with Jeremy don't get any better. Harry and some of his classmates are playing football. But not Jeremy. He's sitting alone under a tree.

"Hey, Jeremy! Why don't you join us?" Macy asks.

"Sure," Jeremy says.

"Great!" Macy says. "You can be on my team."

But instead of playing, Jeremy runs over and steals the ball. "Try playing football now!" he yells.

"Hey!" Ethan cries. "Bring that back!"

"What is up with that kid?" Macy asks.

"I don't know," Harry says. "But as our class superhero, I will save the day. I promise."

Harry finds Jeremy on the other side of the playground.

"That wasn't very nice, Jeremy. Can you please give me the ball back?" Harry asks.

"You'll have to find it first,"
Jeremy says.

Harry does a quick scan of the
playground. He doesn't see the
ball anywhere.

"Why don't you just use your X-ray vision to find the ball, Superman?" Jeremy asks.

That's when Harry remembers he's wearing his superhero flashlight belt! Harry presses the button, and the belt lights up.

"What is that ridiculous thing?" Jeremy asks.

"It's my superhero flashlight belt," Harry replies. "It's going to help me find the ball you took."

"Superhero flashlight belt?" Jeremy laughs. "You are super weird!"

This makes Harry even more determined to find the ball. He shines his belt in the bushes. He immediately spots the ball.

"Found it!" Harry calls to Macy and the other children.

"Whatever," Jeremy says as he walks away.

Harry happily brings the ball back to his friends.

CHAPTER 4

SUPERHERO HARRY WILL SAVE THE DAY

The next day at breaktime, things get even worse. First Jeremy steals Violet's skipping rope and buries it. Then he takes Ethan's hat and hides it in a pile of leaves.

When Harry tries to get back his friends' things, Jeremy teases him. He calls him a nerd because he likes superheroes, science, and inventing stuff.

"We should tell Ms Lane Jeremy is being a bully," Macy says.

"Not yet. Superhero Harry can still save the day," Harry says. "I just need to keep thinking."

* * *

At dinner, Harry is not hungry.

"I forgot the salad dressing," Harry's mum says.

"I'll get it!" Harry says. He runs to the kitchen, and then runs back out.

His mum says, "Please don't run or you'll drop that –"

SPLAT!

Harry cleans up the mess and sits back down.

"What's wrong?" asks his dad.

Harry tells his parents about the mean things Jeremy has been doing and saying.

"Superhero is part of my nickname, but I can't even defend myself or my friends against a bully. What kind of superhero is that?" he asks.

"Have you tried talking to Jeremy?" his mum asks.

"Kind of," Harry says. "He just ignored me. Then he was mean to me again."

"I think you should try again," his dad says.

"If that doesn't work, you need to tell your teacher what's going on," his mum says.

But Harry thinks his parents are wrong. He's sure only one of his superhero inventions can stop Jeremy from being a bully. He has a long night of inventing ahead of him.

CHAPTER 5

BREAKTIME? NO THANKS.

The next day when the bell rings for breaktime, nobody moves.

"Time for breaktime," Ms Lane says.

"No thanks, Ms Lane," Violet says. "I think I'll stay inside and paint a picture."

"I'm going to build a fort," Ethan says. "An inside fort."

"Me too," says Melanie.

"Me three," Jackson says.

Harry and Macy know why their friends don't want to go outside for breaktime.

"So nobody wants to go out for breaktime?" Ms Lane asks, surprised.

They hear a loud thunderclap outside, and then it starts to pour with rain.

"Well," Ms Lane says. "I guess we will have an indoor breaktime today."

"Hooray!" everyone shouts.

Ms Lane says she has to go out for a few minutes. When she's gone, Harry gathers everyone around. Everyone except Jeremy, that is.

"We need to do something," Harry says. "We can't let Jeremy ruin breaktime for us."

"But what can we do?" Violet whispers.

"Yeah, you keep saying you'll save the day," Melanie says. "What's your plan?"

"It's this," Harry says, pulling something from his backpack.

"What is that?" Jackson asks.

"It's my latest superhero invention. I made it using my old bike pump and some confetti," Harry explains.

"Does it work?" Macy asks. "I mean, have you actually tried it on someone?"

"No, but I know it will work. The next time Jeremy does something mean, I'll pump confetti at him. Confetti always puts people in a good mood," Harry says.

"You can't be a bully if you're in a good mood," Macy says.

"Harry, you might actually save the day," Ethan says.

"I sure hope so," Harry says. "After all, I *am* Superhero Harry!"

"What are you guys whispering about?" Jeremy asks.

"Nothing," Macy says.

Jeremy pulls Macy's Wonder
Woman tiara-headband off her
head. He throws it across the
room.

"Why don't you just go away and leave us alone!" Violet yells. "Nobody likes you!"

Harry is about to pump out confetti all over Jeremy. But he stops.

Jeremy is crying.

CHAPTER 6

FROM BULLY
TO FRIEND

"What is going on in here?" Ms Lane asks, walking back into the classroom.

"Everyone is bullying me," Jeremy says.

"That's not true!" Macy yells.

"He's lying!" Harry shouts.

"Calm down, class," Ms Lane says. "Jeremy, are your classmates *really* bullying you?"

Everyone looks at Jeremy. His
face starts turning red. He looks
down at his feet.

"No," Jeremy quietly says. "I've
been bullying them."

"It's never okay to be a bully," Ms Lane says.

"I know. It's just something I do," Jeremy says.

"I made him cry, Ms Lane," Violet says. "I'm really sorry, Jeremy."

"It's fine," Jeremy says.

"All right, class. Let's get back to break and have some fun," Ms Lane says. "Jeremy, please come and see me for a minute."

Harry remembers the advice his parents gave him at dinner. He stops Jeremy.

"Jeremy, why have you been so mean to all of us?" Harry asks.

"My family moves around a lot," he explains. "It's a lot easier to leave if I don't have any friends. I learned that after my third school."

"It must be hard to always be the new kid," Macy says.

"We'd like to be friends with you, no matter how long you stay here," Harry says.

"Really?" Jeremy asks. "You want to be my friend even after I've been bullying you?"

"If you stop being a bully we would love to be your friends," Macy says.

"I'd like that," Jeremy says.

"So would I. Mission complete! Superhero Harry, over and out!"

GLOSSARY

advice opinion about what could or should be done in a situation

bully person who is mean or threatening to others

clumsy moving or doing things in an awkward way and tending to drop or break things

confetti small pieces of colored paper thrown into the air during a celebration

defend make or keep safe from danger

invention useful new device

nickname name given to a person, place, or thing in place of the real name

response written or spoken answer

scan look carefully or examine

sidekick person who helps and spends a lot of time with someone

TALK ABOUT IT

1. Should Harry and his friends have told the teacher about Jeremy being a bully sooner? Why or why not?

2. Harry and his friends tried to include Jeremy, but did they do enough? Talk about your answer.

3. Do you think Jeremy should have been punished for bullying the other children? Why or why not?

WRITE ABOUT IT

1. Pretend you are Jeremy. Write about how you felt after your first day at Harry's school.

2. Jeremy didn't want to be a bully, but he didn't know how else to express his emotions. Make a list of ways you deal with your feelings.

3. Write a paragraph describing what you would do if you were being bullied.

ABOUT THE AUTHOR

Rachel Ruiz is the author of several children's books. She was inspired to write her first picture book, When Penny met POTUS, after working for Barack Obama on his re-election campaign in 2012.

When Rachel isn't writing books, she writes and produces TV shows and documentaries. She lives in Chicago, Illinois, USA, with her husband and their daughter.

ABOUT THE ILLUSTRATOR

Steve May is a professional illustrator and animation director. He says he spent his childhood drawing lots of things and discovering interesting ways of injuring himself.

Steve's work has become a regular feature in the world of children's books. He still draws lots but injures himself less regularly now. He lives in glamourous north London, and his mum says he's a genius.

BE A SUPERHERO AND READ THEM ALL!

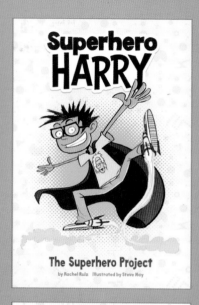

The Superhero Project

by Rachel Ruiz   Illustrated by Steve May

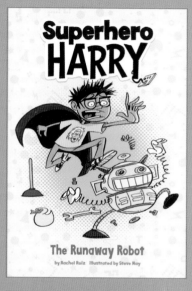

The Runaway Robot

by Rachel Ruiz   Illustrated by Steve May

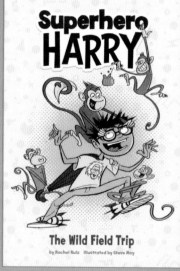

The Wild Field Trip

by Rachel Ruiz   Illustrated by Steve May

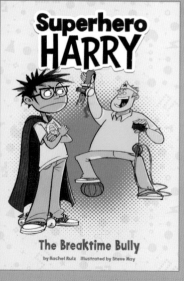

The Breaktime Bully

by Rachel Ruiz   Illustrated by Steve May